Alfie
in the Woods

Debi Gliori

BLOOMSBURY
LONDON OXFORD NEW YORK NEW DELHI SYDNEY

Where's Alfie?

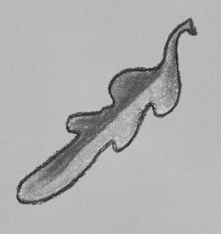

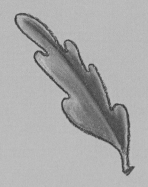

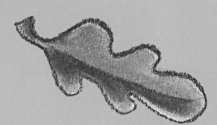

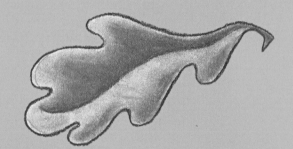

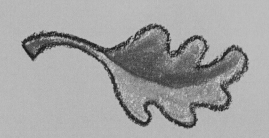

He's gathering treasure
in the woods.

Alfie's playing hide-and-seek
in the trees.

Who-who-who's that?

It's an Alfie-owl
gliding from
tree to tree.

Eeek! Alfie is a fizzy, busy, buzzy
swarm of Alfie-bees flying all around.

Buzzzzzee

Bizzzzzeee

Beeezzzz

Little birds love singing in the Alfie-tree.

Twitter-twitter, tweeet tweeet.

Tweeetery TWEET TWEET.

Sssnuffle rustle, sssnuffle rustle.

Watch out!

Alfie is a stickly prickly hedgehog
rooting through the leaves.

ShhhhHHHHH!
Whatever you do, don't wake
the Alfie-bear curled in his cave.

Oh no! You woke him up!

What's Alfie doing now?

He's helping Daddy carry his treasures home.

For all little bunnies
with big imaginations

Bloomsbury Publishing, London, Oxford, New York, New Delhi and Sydney

First published in Great Britain in 2017 by Bloomsbury Publishing Plc
50 Bedford Square, London WC1B 3DP

This paperback edition first published in 2018

www.bloomsbury.com

BLOOMSBURY is a registered trademark of Bloomsbury Publishing Plc

A CIP catalogue record of this book is available from the British Library

ISBN 978 1 4088 7205 5

All papers used by Bloomsbury Publishing are natural, recyclable products made
from wood grown in well managed forests. The manufacturing processes
conform to the environmental regulations of the country of origin

Printed in China by Leo Paper Products, Heshan, Guangdong

1 3 5 7 9 10 8 6 4 2